THERE
Once
IS A
Queen

First published in the United Kingdom by
HarperCollins *Children's Books* in 2022
HarperCollins *Children's Books* is a division of
HarperCollins *Publishers* Ltd
1 London Bridge Street, London SE1 9GF

www.harpercollins.co.uk

HarperCollins *Publishers*
1st Floor, Watermarque Building, Ringsend Road
Dublin 4, Ireland

1 3 5 7 9 10 8 6 4 2

Text copyright © Michael Morpurgo 2022
Illustrations copyright © Michael Foreman 2022
Cover illustrations copyright © Michael Foreman 2022
Cover design copyright © HarperCollins *Publishers* Ltd 2022
All rights reserved.

ISBN 978-0-00-854161-3

Michael Morpurgo and Michael Foreman assert the moral right
to be identified as the author and illustrator of the work respectively.

A CIP catalogue record for this title is available from the British Library.

Printed and bound by CPI Group (UK) Ltd, Croydon, CR0 4YY.

MIX
Paper from
responsible sources
FSC™ C007454

michael morpurgo

THERE Once IS A Queen

illustrated by
Michael Foreman

HarperCollins *Children's Books*

Foreword

There once was a little girl, a princess, who never expected to be queen. But then, when she was very young, she did become queen, our queen. It was she whose life and work inspired me to sit down and write this story. She has been queen for longer than any other queen – or king, come to that – of this country. All my life, she has been there, been part of the landscape of our lives, a constant and reassuring presence in a rapidly changing and often unsettling world.

I very much wanted my story to play a small part in the
celebration of the Queen's Platinum Jubilee in June of
2022. There was another Queen Elizabeth some time ago,
a cousin fourteen times removed to our own queen.
A great writer, Edmund Spenser, once wrote a long poem
for her that he called *The Faerie Queene*. My story is not
a poem, and not long, but, as you will discover, it is also
about a fairy queen – although spelled differently.

Michael Foreman and I should like to dedicate this book
        to Her Majesty The Queen, in gratitude,
in affection and in admiration.

There once is a queen.

Not a fairytale
nor a
faerie queene.

But **our** queen.

Once upon a time, there was a little girl. One day, they say, she planted a tree with her papa, an oak tree. Quite soon, that tree was higher than she was.

And quite soon after that

she discovered she was a princess.

She didn't feel like a princess. She would go and sit on the grass under the branches of her oak tree, and was always happy there, just being a girl, and not a princess at all.

Princesses were in books;

her life was going to be her own story.

She loved the countryside, the hills and the trees
and the rivers, and the animals above everything —
all animals.

Butterflies and beetles,
swifts and swallows
and hovering hawks.

Best of all the animals for her was her beloved horse. (But don't whisper that near her corgis.) Whenever she went to saddle her horse to go for a ride, she would reach up and lay her hand on his neck,

which felt to her like warm velvet.

She would talk to that horse
like she talked to no one else.
He was her best friend.

Then while she was still young there came
a terrible war, like a storm raging through the skies,
leaving behind lives destroyed, cities and towns in ruins.
And with it there came over the country a great wave of
sadness, and people wherever they were, whoever they
were, just had to carry on, somehow, and they did.
The news came, good and bad, victory and defeat, but for
the princess and the people life and sorrow went on.

She put on a uniform like millions of others and mended
engines on cars and trucks. She was always good at that.
The people tried to be brave.

She tried to be brave.

Then, on the day when the war was over at last,
and done and won, the princess went to sit under her tree,
the swifts and swallows skimming the air above her,
shrieking in their joy.

That night, the princess crept out of her palace, which she was not really supposed to do, and danced in the streets in amongst the crowds, and had a fine old time in amongst the people. And no one knew who she was.

She was one of them, a girl again,

not a princess.

But by this time she had become quite used to being a princess. She may not always have liked it, because people were always looking at her, and that wasn't easy.

She knew that sooner or later a princess finds a handsome prince, and they get married – she liked that idea anyway, so long as she could choose her prince.

And sure enough,

sooner rather than later,

that's what happened.

But she still loved to be alone sometimes,
to go riding on her horse, to sit in the grass under her
oak tree that grew taller every year, where the branches
were spreading out ever wider, ever higher, above her head.
Here she would still look for butterflies and beetles,
and swifts and swallows
and hovering hawks.

Here she could have her time to dream, be a girl again,
think her thoughts, feel the wind on her face.
That tree became her thinking tree, her dreaming tree.
Here she tried to work out what her life was for, and decided
she had to do whatever she could, work as hard as she could,
to make life better not for herself
but for the people.

She was happier in these young days
than she had ever been, and with good reason.
As well as being a princess with her handsome
prince at her side, she had become
the mother of her first child,
a little boy.

A while later, she was away with her prince,
travelling in Africa and seeing in the wild, for the first time,
so many of the wonderful animals she had seen and loved
only in pictures and stories since she was a child:
elephants, giraffes, lions, baboons
and once even a rhinoceros.

These were truly the best of times.

But while she was away there came the saddest
news of her life. Her dear papa had died suddenly.
So now she wasn't a princess any more,

but a queen, and a queen not just of one country

but of lots of countries

all over the world.

She needed her
thinking tree
more than
ever now.

So this little girl, this princess,
this wife and mother was crowned queen
in front of her whole family, in a great abbey,
with the whole world watching
on black-and-white television . . .

. . . with great crowds thronging the streets,

    cheering her in the rain, as she rode back to her palace

        in her gleaming golden carriage,

            her handsome prince at her side.

There might have been grey clouds and the rain,

but for that day at least the people could forget their troubles.

They had a young and beautiful queen with a radiant smile

that warmed their hearts.

It felt to them like a new age being born,

that **everything** would be **better**,

would be all right.

And it was, in so many ways it was. Everywhere, people were busy trying to make the best of this new world, a world of new ideas, new inventions, new energy, a time of rebuilding, of festivals and fun, a time for creating books for everyone, and making plays in new theatres and making music in new concert halls and clubs, of climbing mountains, running under-four-minute miles, if you could, of sailing round the world in yachts.

A new day was being born.

There were soon more schools and teachers for all the
children, and better schools too – this new queen opened
many of them herself and visited hundreds of them.
There were more nurses and doctors,
and more hospitals too,
for everyone.

And in the middle of all this she had three more babies of her own and, as if this wasn't enough, she gathered around her so many corgis she couldn't even count them.

But, happy as she was, she still needed to be away from everything and everyone, and have time to remember who she was, and there was only one place to do that: under her thinking tree, from where a blackbird would often sing to her.

She loved that.

One day, under her tree, she thought the thought that stays with her to this day.

Never forget, she told herself,
everyone matters.

Then she spoke it aloud to her corgis.

"Never let me forget, corgis: everyone matters."
They gave her a look as if to say, "Who do you think you are? The queen or something?"
That was why she loved her corgis so much – and her horses, come to that. To them she was always that little girl again. And she knew it.

But, of course, the work went on.
She launched ships, opened workplaces
and new towns,

and housing estates, shopping centres and parks and factories.

In time, the water was becoming cleaner in the rivers,

the air too in the cities was soon

cleaner to breathe.

It was very far from a perfect world,
but it was beginning to be a fairer, brighter world.
And wherever she went the people cheered and waved,
loving to see her because they knew
that their young queen cared,

that she was doing her very best, working as hard as
she could to make it a better, happier world for everyone.

Anyone she stopped to talk to

never forgot the moment.

She went all around the world
and treated every country and all the
people there as one big family.
And everywhere – at home and
over the seas – the glowing
smile went with her, a smile
of goodwill, of reconciliation.

Queen she was and is, but seen
more and more, as the years
passed, not as a monarch who
"rules over" them, which she
knows she never has been anyway,
but more as a mother to them,
a grandmother, and now
a great-grandmother.

She has met and advised and befriended
more prime ministers and presidents and kings
and queens and emperors than anyone has had
hot dinners, dined and even danced with some
of them, and treated them all as if they matter too,

because they do,

but no more than anyone else.

This world has been changing fast about her,
old ways fading away, a new tide of openness, of inclusiveness,
was sweeping in, new technologies endlessly reinventing
themselves, changing our way of being, and she has adapted
to them, embracing them when she saw they were good.

The times she'd been born into have gone. She looks to the
future, remembering the best of the past, and acknowledging
the worst, her words healing, full of hope and of grandmotherly
wisdom, and always calling for greater knowledge and
understanding, and for harmony between peoples
and faiths and cultures.

She knows how precious peace is,
        how important are our rights and our freedom,
    how we treat one another
                and the world about us.

And she's always there when needed,
seeing the people through triumph and tragedy,

standing beside them

through sorrow and pain and joy . . .

. . . speaking truth from
her heart.

Back home, with her own family growing up
around her, she might go out riding less these days,
but she still goes to sit under her oak tree,

　　　her thinking tree,

　　　　　　her dreaming tree,

the one she planted all those years before, and to rest
under its shade, remembering the girl she was,
before she was ever a queen, a wife

　　　　　or a mother or a grandmother.

She remembers her handsome prince – sadly, sadly
no longer with her – and family and friends now gone.

And she looks out again for the butterflies and beetles,

　　　　　the swifts and the swallows

　　　　　　　　and the hovering hawks.

And, family apart, little brings her greater joy than to stand by a beloved horse, her hand resting on his neck, still feeling like warm velvet.

(But, for goodness' sake, don't whisper a word of this to the corgis.
Pembrokeshire corgis, by the way. They are the drovers' dogs of old,
who drove cattle and sheep hundreds of miles to market:
working dogs, proper dogs. Dogs for a queen and for a little girl.)

She has done her best, endured – as everyone
must – difficult times, and come through,
        done her work, and goes on doing it.
She has shown the way, encouraged and helped everyone
to do the same, left the people in no doubt that they matter.
        No more could be asked of anyone.

There once is a queen ever constant to her people,
familiar as family, but not simply a face on a banknote,
not always being royal – though she's good enough at that –
        but best at being herself.

That crown of hers looks heavy, never easy to balance.
        Didn't Shakespeare say it?
                "Uneasy lies the head that wears a crown"?

Under her great oak tree, she is never uneasy.
She's much more herself, wearing her scarf not her crown,
with her herd of corgis scurrying around her, a whole
people's favourite granny.

Probably, definitely, the most admired granny-queen
in the **entire** world.

She's no faerie queene.

Better by far.
She's **our** queen,
our granny-queen.

'Bless her heart.